For Carrie, with love and happy memories of Mersea.

A TEMPLAR BOOK
First published in the UK in 2006 by Templar Publishing,
an imprint of The Templar Company plc,
Pippbrook Mill, London Road, Dorking, Surrey, RH4 1JE, UK
www.templarco.co.uk

Text and illustration copyright © 2006 by Liane Payne

1 3 5 7 9 10 8 6 4 2

ISBN-13: 978-1-84011-372-3
ISBN-10: 1-84011-372-3

Designed by Caroline Reeves
Edited by Sue Harris

Printed in China

a goodnight warren book

Warren and the Sandcastle

Liane Payne

templar publishing

It's a beautiful summer's evening and Warren the rabbit is visiting his Aunt May and Uncle Albert. They are taking him on a day trip tomorrow and Warren can't wait to see where they are going. As Aunt May packs a tasty picnic lunch, Warren tries to find out more. "It's a surprise, Warren, so you'll just have to wait and see!" Aunt May says with a smile.

Early the next day, Warren and his friends, Gus and Pippy, find Uncle Albert loading the car. "Hop in!" says Uncle Albert.

As the little car chugs along, Warren asks if they are nearly there. Aunt May says, "Almost. Have you guessed where we're going yet?"

"The seaside!" shouts Warren. "This is the best surprise ever!"

"We knew you'd enjoy it," says Uncle Albert, smiling.

Ice Creams

Warren leaps out of the car and jumps onto the soft sand. "Come on!" he says to Pippy and Gus. "Let's go exploring." Changing into their swimsuits as fast as they can, the friends gather up their net, buckets and beach ball and head off.

While the friends are playing a ball game, Warren spots a little sandcastle. "Let's build the biggest sandcastle ever seen!" he cries. So they set to work.

"It's jolly good," says Pippy, as they stand back to admire their handiwork. "But it needs shells and pebbles to make it look really spectacular."

Warren and his friends search everywhere, but they can't find any shells. Just then a seagull swoops down and asks, "Have you seen a baby crab? His name's Nipper and his Mummy and Daddy can't find him." Although Warren really wants to finish decorating his sandcastle, he smiles and says, "We'll help you to find Nipper."

Warren decides to go and ask Aunt May
and Uncle Albert if they've seen Nipper.
But Aunt May shakes her head. "Sorry, Warren.
I've not seen any crabs today," she says.
Opening an eye, Uncle Albert suggests they
should go and check the rock pools. "That's
where I'd hide if I were a crab," he says.
Warren, Pippy and Gus hurry off.
"Poor Nipper. I hope we find him soon," says
Warren as they run along to the rock pools.

The friends are searching among the slippery rocks when Warren spots something orange. "It's Nipper!" he says. "Look, he's sound asleep. Let's go and tell Aunt May he's safe."

Aunt May says they should have their picnic to celebrate, but Warren wants to finish the sandcastle first. When the friends go back, they gasp. The sandcastle's covered in lots of shiny shells. "Wow!" says Warren. "It's the best sandcastle ever! But who found the shells and decorated it?"

"We did!" says Nipper. "To thank you for finding him," adds the Gull. Aunt May asks Warren's new friends to share the picnic she has prepared. "Tuck in," she says. Uncle Albert treats them all to ice cream and Aunt May takes a photo of the friends with their splendid sandcastle.

As the sun begins to set, it's time to say goodbye to their new friends and head home. "Come back soon!" calls Nipper. "We will!" promises Warren.

"Next time, I'll ask Nipper to show us where he found those lovely shells," thinks Warren, as he falls asleep. Goodnight Warren!